This project is sponsored by
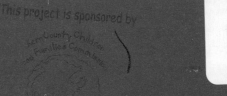

Funded by Proposition 10

D0116080

E   McPhail,
McP   David M.
              Edward in
           the jungle

RATH

AUG 1 4 2002

DAVID McPHAIL

EDWARD
IN THE
JUNGLE

DAVID McPHAIL

EDWARD
IN THE
JUNGLE

Little, Brown and Company
Boston New York London

For Tris and Kathy
and for
Howard and Tracy
Lee and Rachel
Hector and Marilyn
and their beautiful children
Love,
D.

OTHER BOOKS FEATURING EDWARD:

Santa's Book of Names
Edward and the Pirates

Copyright © 2002 by David McPhail

All rights reserved. No part of this book may be reproduced in any form or by any electronic or mechanical means, including information storage and retrieval systems, without permission in writing from the publisher, except by a reviewer who may quote brief passages in a review.

First Edition

Tarzan® is a registered trademark used by permission of Edgar Rice Burroughs, Inc.

Library of Congress Cataloging-in-Publication Data

McPhail, David.
  Edward in the jungle / David McPhail. — 1st ed.
   p. cm.
  Summary: Edward loves to read about Tarzan, Lord of the Jungle, and one afternoon he becomes so
  absorbed in his book that he finds himself deep in Tarzan's jungle.
  ISBN 0-316-56391-9
  [1. Imagination — Fiction. 2. Tarzan (Fictitious character) — Fiction. 3. Jungle animals — Fiction.]
I. Title.
PZ7.M2427 Ei 2001
[E] — dc21   00-062440

10 9 8 7 6 5 4 3 2 1

TWP

Printed in Singapore

The illustrations were done in acrylic on watercolor board.
The text was set in Caslon 224, and the display type is Decotura.

Edward loved to read. He especially loved to read adventure stories.

His favorite stories were about Tarzan, Lord of the Jungle.

Tarzan was raised by the Great Gray Apes, and he grew up to become their leader.

All of the animals loved him (except the crocodiles) and would come to his aid whenever he called.

Edward had a set of animals just like the animals in Tarzan's jungle (without the zebra).

One day, Edward took his animals into the jungle behind his house.

He spread them out around him, then lay back on the cool moss and opened another Tarzan adventure.

Edward was so absorbed in his reading that he didn't notice
what was happening. . . .

When he finally looked up, an enormous crocodile was coming toward him.

The crocodile lunged at Edward, but at that instant Edward
was snatched out of the way by none other than Tarzan himself,
and a moment later they were swinging through the trees on a
sturdy vine.

When they were a safe distance from the crocodile, Tarzan landed on the branch of a large tree and set Edward down.

"I'll teach you what to do if you need help and I'm not around," said Tarzan. Then he tipped back his head and yelled the loudest yell that Edward had ever heard—a booming call that echoed through every part of the jungle.

Immediately the branches around them filled up with all manner of birds, monkeys, snakes, and climbing cats.

On the ground, a huge elephant appeared and was soon joined by every other kind of animal that Edward had ever read about.

Tarzan raised his hand, and all the animals grew quiet. "This is our new friend," he announced. "Watch over him!"

Tarzan waved his arm, and the animals disappeared as quickly as they had arrived.

"I have to go pull a stuck hippo out of the mud," Tarzan told Edward. "Wait here." Then he grabbed a vine and swung away.

Edward looked around. Crouched on the branch below him was a leopard, and standing on the ground beneath the leopard was a small antelope.

Edward leaned over and tried to warn the antelope without disturbing the big cat.

"*Pssst* — run — run for your life!" he whispered. But he had leaned too far. He lost his grip and went tumbling out of the tree, past the wide-eyed leopard, and — *PLOP!* — right onto the back of the antelope.

The antelope was so startled that it galloped away as fast as it could go, with Edward's arms wrapped tightly around its neck. It raced along the riverbank, leaping fallen logs and charging through tangled thickets.

Suddenly the antelope stopped short and Edward went flying. He landed in the soft moss of the riverbank — in the exact same spot where he had first met the crocodile.

The crocodile was still there, but he was completely tied up, and two men were loading him into their boat.

Serves him right, thought Edward. *That crocodile is no friend of mine.*

But then Edward's heart softened. As unfriendly as the crocodile was, he didn't deserve to be bound and dragged away from his river home.

Edward stepped forward. "Let him go!" he said to the men. When the men looked up and saw Edward, they laughed. "And what will you do if we don't?" said one of the men.

"This is what I will do," said Edward, and he drew a deep breath and tried to yell just the way Tarzan had taught him.

But instead of a mighty yell, a squeaky noise came out of Edward's mouth.

So Edward tried again. This time a powerful sound poured out of him and echoed through the jungle.

The men stopped laughing, and from the silence that followed, new sounds emerged — the sounds of wings flapping and hooves pounding.

Immediately the trees were filled with all kinds of creatures,

and a circle of animals surrounded the two men.

"Now will you let the crocodile go?" Edward asked.

The men dropped the crocodile — *SPLASH!* — jumped
into their boat, and sped off.

Edward untied the rope that bound the great beast, and

without a word of thanks, the crocodile slowly swam away.

"You did a good thing," said Tarzan, as he swung down and landed beside Edward.

While the two stood watching the crocodile, something caught Edward's eye.

He saw the top of his house appear above the trees on the other side of the river.

He could see his bedroom window with its jungle-patterned curtains.

Edward looked up at Tarzan.
"If I had a boat," Tarzan said, "I could take you home."

Just then the crocodile turned around and started swim-
ming back.

"I think he wants to help," said Tarzan.

Edward climbed onto the crocodile and sat down.

The crocodile paddled off, and when they got to the opposite
bank, Edward leaped ashore. He turned to say thank you, but
the crocodile had sunk out of sight.

As he started up the path to his house, Edward thought he heard Tarzan's yell.

But it was just his father calling him home for dinner.